Mowgli liked living in the man-village most of the time. He lived with Ranjan's family and his best friend was Shanti. They had lots of fun together, except when he and Ranjan played tricks on Shanti, which made her cross.

Sometimes though, Mowgli missed his old life in the jungle. Most of all he missed his good friend Baloo the bear.

One day, Mowgli was singing, dancing and having fun with his friends in the village. As they danced, they wandered near the jungle. Ranjan's father heard them. "The jungle is a dangerous place," he scolded, showing Mowgli the marks a tiger had once made on his arm.

In the
jungle the
big bear, Baloo,
missed Mowgli,
too. "It's not safe for
him in the jungle," said wise Bagheera, the
panther. "Shere Khan is looking for Mowgli."

Mowgli had once made a fool of the tiger,
who was set on revenge. Baloo didn't care,
and soon found a way to outwit his friends
to get to the man-village, and Mowgli.

As night fell, Baloo reached the village and found his friend, but the big bear didn't know Shere Khan was in the village too.

Poor Shanti was shocked to see Mowgli with a bear! "Wild animal!" she screamed.

Baloo picked up Mowgli and ran. The villagers saw only Shere Khan and drove him back to the jungle.

Shanti ran towards the jungle after Mowgli, and Ranjan followed.

Shere Khan was angry. How could that stupid bear have got to Mowgli before him? Silently, he crept up on Kaa the snake. "Where's the man-cub," he asked furiously. "At the ssswamp," lied Kaa, desperate to escape with his life.

The villagers searched desperately for the lost children, scaring the jungle animals as they passed nearby. Wise Bagheera had an idea that Baloo might know something. "Have you seen the boy?" he asked the big bear.

"Wish I could help you, Baggy," smiled Baloo, hiding his friend, Mowgli.

Baloo took Mowgli to a secret hiding place. The monkeys there had a great time making fun of the man-village. Mowgli didn't enjoy that, and wandered off.

After hours of searching, Shanti at last found Mowgli, at the same moment as Baloo, who had come looking for him. Seeing Shanti, Baloo roared! Bravely, she bopped him on the nose!

Mowgli tried to explain, but Shanti was angry and stormed off with Ranjan. Mowgli followed, but when he reached her, Shere Khan was there! "Run!" Mowgli cried.

Shanti and Ranjan hid as Mowgli raced on, with Shere Khan close behind. "Ranjan, wait here. I've got to help Mowgli," she whispered, and hurried on to find her friend.

Little Ranjan tried to follow her but he was too little to keep up. Luckily, Baloo was close by, and asked Bagheera to look after him.

Next, Shanti bumped into Baloo! "Hey! I'm here to help Mowgli," they both said together, a little crossly.

"I guess we're on the same side," said Baloo in a more friendly way. They rushed on together.

Mowgli led Shere Khan to some ruins. Shanti and Baloo soon arrived, and they all tried desperately to hide from and confuse Shere Khan. Suddenly, he pounced, chasing them onto an ancient stone tiger. The mighty Shere Khan was too heavy and CRACK! The huge monument gave way.

Shere Khan fell, and the head of the great stone tiger fell too, trapping him inside. There was no way out.

Shanti and Mowgli were safe at last. Outside, they were reunited with Ranjan, who rushed to meet the villagers with Shanti.

Mowgli didn't know whether to stay, or go back with the others. But Baloo knew he belonged in the man-village. "You better hurry," he said gently, hugging his friend as Bagheera watched sadly.

"I'll miss you Papa Bear," whispered Mowgli as he ran to join the others.

Life was soon back to normal in the man-village, almost. Now, whenever Mowgli and his friends went for water, they crept right into the jungle! Then, they called Baloo and danced to that crazy jungle beat, all friends together at last.